D1385250

The CHRISTMAS Bear

The CHRISTMAS *Bear*

ANNE MANGAN *and* JOANNE MOSS

SCHOLASTIC INC.

New York   Toronto   London   Auckland   Sydney
Mexico City   New Delhi   Hong Kong   Buenos Aires

It was nearly Christmas, and it was snowing.
Inside the shop, among all the other toys, a little
bear was delighted. He was a polar bear and loved
snow.
Now that it was Christmas, he hoped he would get
a home at last. He had been waiting a long time. He
was sure someone would spot him in the window
and want a bear to match the Christmas snow, but
he was passed by every time.

"Someone must want me," thought the little bear gleefully, when he felt himself being lifted from the window—until he heard the shop assistant mutter, "That bear won't sell. He's taking up good window space."

The little bear was put on a high shelf inside the shop, to make room for a cute pink teddy. He sat there between a yellow monkey and a big doll.

"The longer you're in the shop the higher you go," whispered the monkey. "We're all forgotten now. Children look on the lower shelves."
"Why wasn't I sold?" asked the little polar bear.

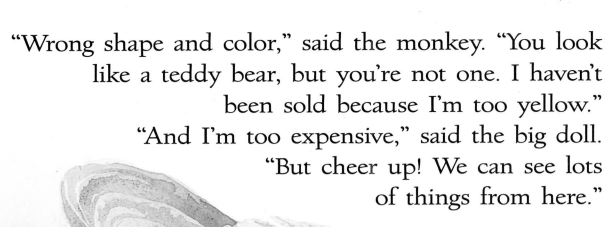

"Wrong shape and color," said the monkey. "You look like a teddy bear, but you're not one. I haven't been sold because I'm too yellow."
"And I'm too expensive," said the big doll.
"But cheer up! We can see lots of things from here."

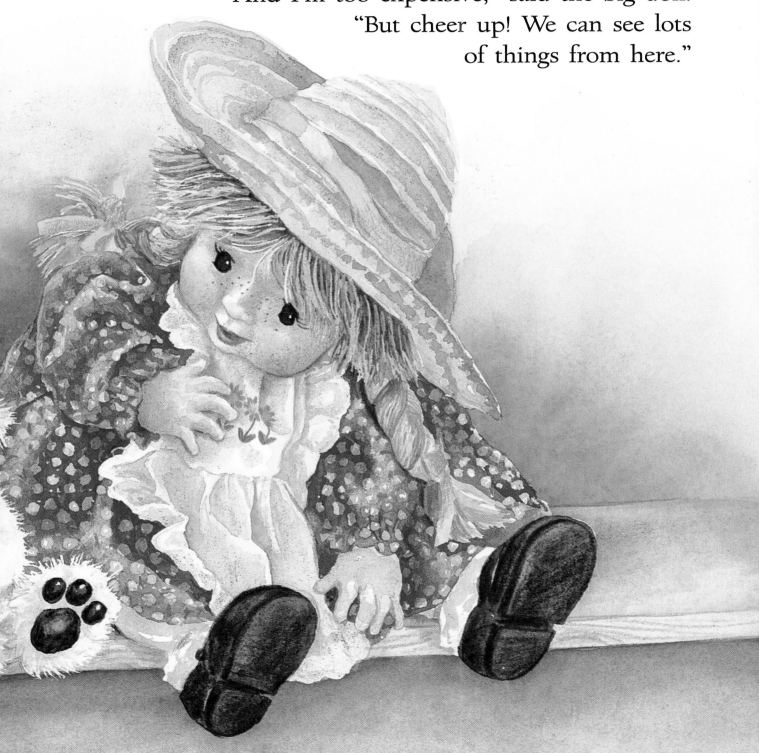

The shop looked very cheerful with all the Christmas decorations, but a shop wasn't like a home, the little bear thought. He began to feel quite dizzy.

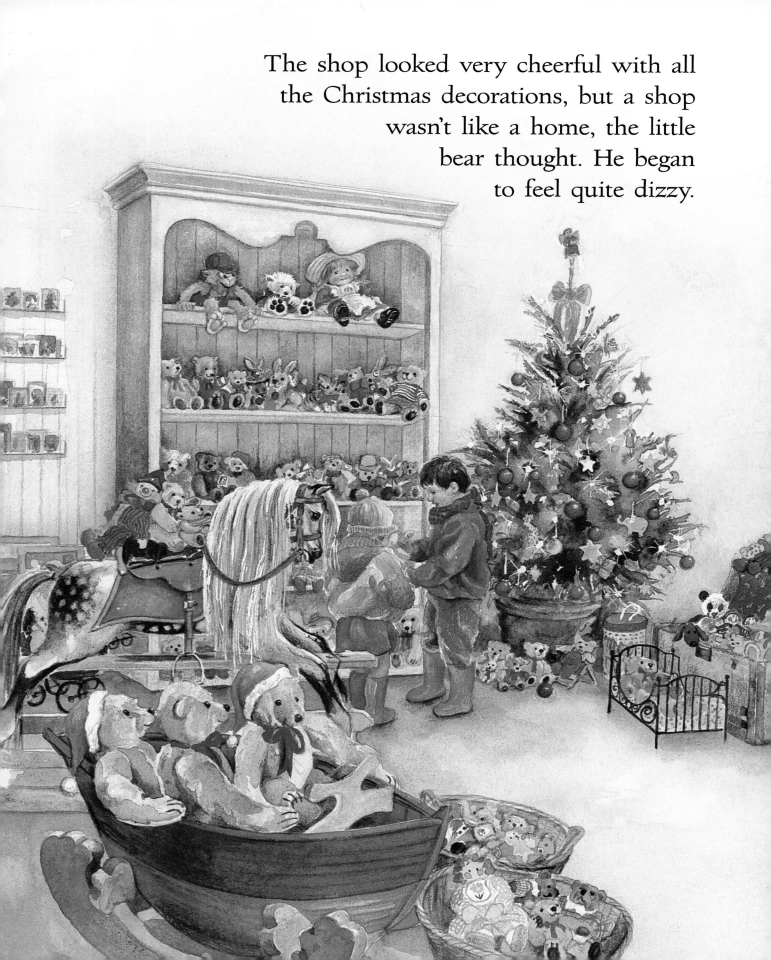

"I know. I've got an idea," said the monkey—and he wriggled off the shelf, right into a child's arms!

"You could do that," the doll told the little polar bear. "I'd be too afraid," he said. "I wouldn't dare either," said the doll. "I would break." So the big beautiful doll and the little polar bear sat side by side and waited and hoped. . . .

A week before Christmas a lady and a little boy came into the shop to buy a present for his sister. "Becky already has lots of dolls," he said. "Let's get something different."
The little polar bear's heart lifted. He certainly was different. The assistant reached up and took him down off the high shelf.

"He looks like a mistake," said the lady rudely.
"People will think we got him cheap."
They chose a calculator instead.

The little bear felt his insides sagging.
It was terrible to be a mistake.
He flopped right over, and
someone picked him up,
gave him a shake,
and set him back
in his place.

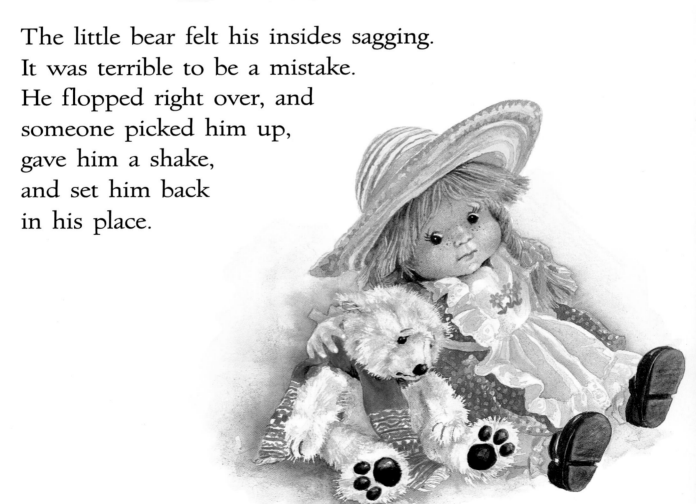

The next day a girl came into the shop. She wanted a pretty toy to sit in her room and look nice. She saw the doll on the high shelf. "It's exactly what I've been looking for," she cried. The big doll was overjoyed. She didn't want to be hugged and loved as the little polar bear did. She just wanted to look pretty.

The little polar bear missed the big doll very much. He sat on his high shelf all alone, while people came in and out of the shop in a last-minute rush to buy their presents for Christmas.
He saw so many toys being sold, and he wanted a home more than ever. If only someone would choose him!

It seemed as if the little polar bear's wish would
be granted, because suddenly someone looked
up at him and said, "What a cute little bear. I'll
take him for my youngest. It's her birthday today."
The little polar bear was delighted. He didn't
mind being bumped along in a bag, all the way
to his new home.

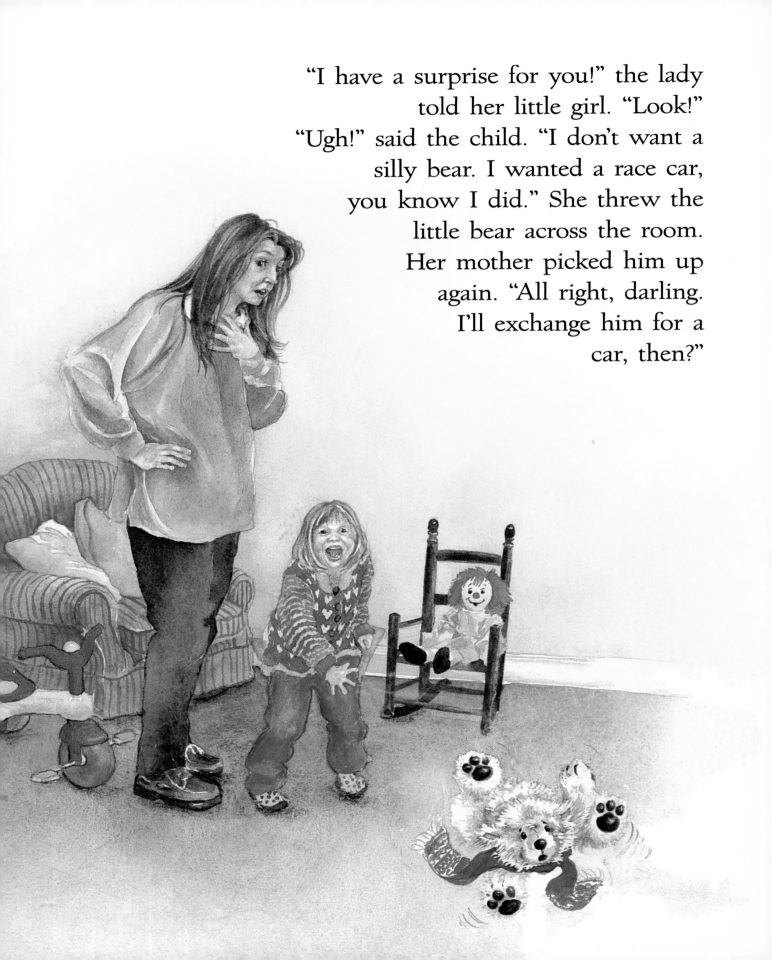

"I have a surprise for you!" the lady told her little girl. "Look!"
"Ugh!" said the child. "I don't want a silly bear. I wanted a race car, you know I did." She threw the little bear across the room. Her mother picked him up again. "All right, darling. I'll exchange him for a car, then?"

The little polar bear was
bumped all the way back
to the shop and put
up on the high shelf
once more.

He felt worse than ever.

He had given up
all hope of ever
being wanted
and loved.

On Christmas Eve a man and a woman with friendly faces came into the shop.
"We'd like to buy a Christmas present for our niece," said the woman.
"A doll?" asked the assistant.
"Well, I don't know if she likes dolls," said the man.
"Some do and some don't."
The man was so tall that he could see the high shelf easily. He noticed the little polar bear at once.

"How about this little fellow, Nicole?" said the man, taking down the polar bear. "He's nice and soft. And snow-white like the North Pole."
"Yes, I think Elly will like him, Nicholas. Let's buy him."

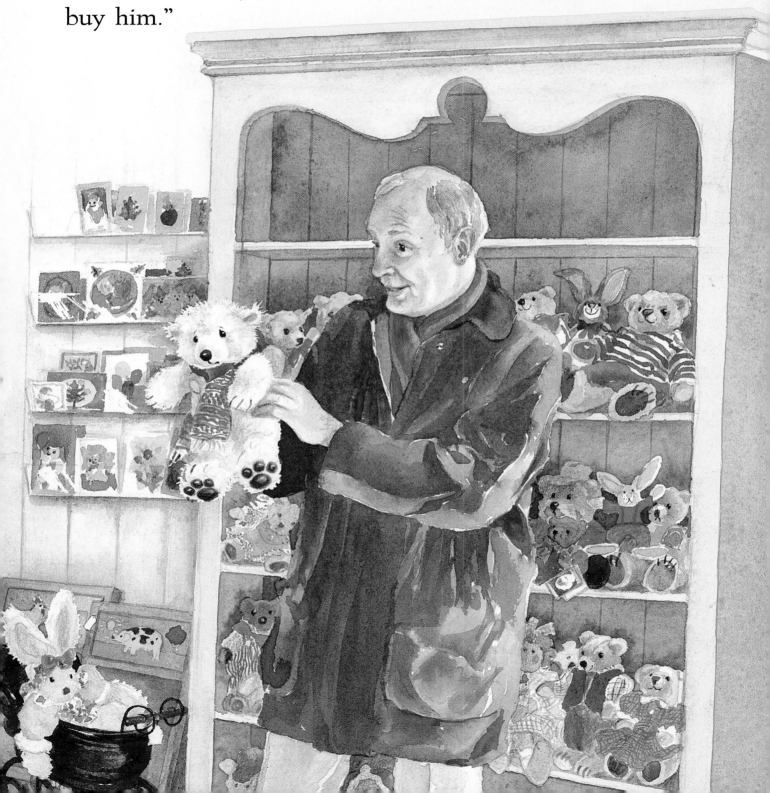

The little polar bear felt happy and afraid, all at the same time. "Suppose Elly doesn't like me?" he thought. "Suppose she thinks I'm a mistake? Suppose she wants a race car instead?" He worried and worried as he was wrapped up in a Christmas package for the next day.

On Christmas morning, Uncle Nicholas and Aunt Nicole arrived at Elly's home. "We have an extra-special present for you, Elly," said Uncle Nicholas. Elly felt the package. It was soft, like something she wanted to hug.

Then she opened it. Elly looked at the little bear, and the little bear looked at Elly. "Do you like him?" asked Aunt Nicole.

Elly picked up the little bear and hugged him.
She buried her face in his soft fur.
"Oh, yes," she cried. "He's the best present
I ever got. I'll name him Nicky, after both of you."
Elly took Nicky outside to let him see the snow.
Now the little polar bear had a home and a
name and someone to give him lots and
lots of hugs. He was the happiest
little bear in the world!

For Nick Cholis,
Nicholas P. Bear & Elly Roach
~A.M.

For Miles & Bruin
~J.M.

ISBN 0-439-70788-9

Text copyright © 1999 by Anne Mangan. Illustrations copyright © 1999 by Joanne Moss. All rights reserved.
Published by Scholastic Inc., 557 Broadway, New York, NY 10012, by arrangement with Little Tiger Press.
SCHOLASTIC, TROLL, and associated logos and designs are trademarks and/or registered trademarks of Scholastic Inc.

12 11 10 9 8 7 6 5 4 3 2 1   4 5 6 7 8 9/0

Printed in the U.S.A.   40

First Scholastic printing, November 2004